Wrong Way

Mark Macleod • Judith Rossell

Kane Miller
A DIVISION OF EDC PUBLISHING

For Halcyon and Sam and a cold walk in Denmark, with love — Dad

For Rupert — JR

First American Edition 2012
Kane Miller, A Division of EDC Publishing

First published in English in Sydney, Australia, by HarperCollins Publishers Australia Pty Limited in 2010. This
North American edition is published by arrangement with HarperCollins Publishers Australia Pty Limited.

Text copyright © Mark Macleod 2010
Illustrations copyright © Judith Rossell 2010

The author and Illustrator have asserted their right to be identified as the author and illustrator of this work.

For information contact:
Kane Miller, A Division of EDC Publishing
PO Box 470663
Tulsa, OK 74147-0663
www.kanemiller.com
www.edcpub.com

Library of Congress Control Number: 2011929947

Printed and bound in China by RR Donnelley

1 2 3 4 5 6 7 8 9 10

ISBN: 978-1-61067-077-7

Right Way and Your Way
were no trouble at all.
They listened to their mother
and did whatever she said.

But Wrong Way always wanted
to do things differently.

And that was what happened when their
mother decided to teach them all to swim.
"We're off to the pond this morning,"
she said, "and it's quite a walk.
So pay attention and follow me."

While the other children flip-flopped
along behind her in a nice straight line,
Wrong Way sat down in the middle of the path.

"We walk first, and *then* we take a rest,"
said their mother. "Let's get a move on!"

"My legs are bored," Wrong Way said.
"I want to be carried."

His mother looked up at the
clouds and sighed. "You're too
big to be carried," she said.
"Come on. Let's get moving!"

And off she went.

Right Way and Your Way walked in a nice straight line behind her. But Wrong Way had dived into the bushes after a big, juicy snail.

"Leave that here," said his mother.
"There'll be plenty of time for lunch *after*
we've had our swim. Come on. Follow me."

She set off again with the other two,
but Wrong Way had noticed a puddle
and couldn't wait to get his feet wet.

"At this rate, we'll never
make it to the pond,"
said their mother.

"I'd better carry you, I suppose. But your job is to watch where we're going. All right?"

Wrong Way hopped up onto her back, but instead of looking straight ahead, he turned around to watch the other two.

"Why does he get to be so special?"
said Right Way and Your Way.

Wrong Way grinned down at
them and popped the snail into
his mouth with a little quack.
Then he gave his bottom a short wiggle.

Soon they came to the end of the path.

Right Way, Your Way
and their mother
looked to the right,

and to the left,

then to the right again.

Suddenly there was a honk from someone
louder and bossier than a goose!

The ducklings and their mother flapped
to the other side of the road just in time.

But Wrong Way didn't look

and was blown

and tossed

and tumbled, over and over

and landed
on his back
upside down.

Where was everyone?

"We're not stopping for you this time," said a voice far away. "So you'd better get a move on if you want to catch up."

All Wrong Way could
see were three tails wagging
busily in the distance.

"Wait for me!" he cried.
"I'm only little."

Catching up seemed to take forever.

But there, at last, by the edge of the pond,
were Right Way and Your Way,

shivering
— just a bit.

"Now," their mother was saying,

"you slide into the water gently.

Then kick your legs as fast as you can."

Wrong Way was so pleased to
see them that he rushed over,
quacking and flapping his wings.
"Look at me!" he shouted.

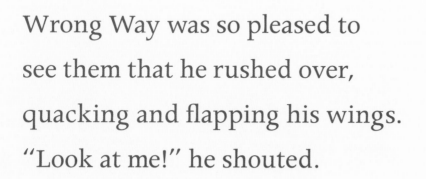

He ran right past them,

sailed straight up overhead

and came down with a loud splash.

When the water was still once again, Wrong Way
noticed that he was right out in the middle
of the pond and couldn't see the bottom.

It was dark and deep and cold.

Looking up, he saw that his mother had pushed out onto the pond, with the other ducklings behind her.

"We wondered where you'd gotten to," she said.

Wrong Way flipped onto his back,
then he swam over and joined them.

His mother shrugged.
"That's the wrong way to
cross the pond," she said.

"It's just different."
Wrong Way laughed.
"And it's fun!"

His mother watched him and smiled.

"I think we'd better call you My Way.

Now let's get a move on!

Follow me, all of you," she said.

And they did —
across the pond
in a nice straight line.